Ghost Dogs

and Animals of the West

Ghost Dogs

and Animals of the West

by June Reynolds

ReadersMagnet, LLC

Ghost Dogs and Animals of the West
Copyright © 2018 by June Reynolds

Published in the United States of America
ISBN Paperback: 978-1-948864-92-3
ISBN Hardback: 978-1-948864-93-0
ISBN eBook: 978-1-948864-94-7

All rights reserved. No part of this publication may be reproduced, stored in a retrieval system or transmitted in any way by any means, electronic, mechanical, photocopy, recording or otherwise without the prior permission of the author except as provided by USA copyright law.

The opinions expressed by the author are not necessarily those of ReadersMagnet, LLC.

ReadersMagnet, LLC
10620 Treena Street, Suite 230 | San Diego, California, 92131 USA
1.619. 354. 2643 | www.readersmagnet.com

Book design copyright © 2018 by ReadersMagnet, LLC. All rights reserved.
Cover design by Ericka Walker
Interior design by Shemaryl Evans
Illustrated by Clyde List
Photos by June Reynolds

Contents

Preface 7
The Common Mourning Dove 9
Falling from a Dark Sky 10
Chocolate Brown Rabbits... 12
Little Brown Fox Knows... 14
Shadow and Shade... 15
Sentinel Cow 16
Owls 18
Coyote 21
Proud Bird 25
Up the North Umpqua 26
Surprise in the Meadow... 28
The Chicken Feeding Song 31
Big Creek Pigeons 32
Oregon Bear 34
Message 37
Devil Dog of Rex Hill 38
Dark Raven and the New Ocean 42
The Peccary Parade 45
The Black Lizard.. 48
Sheep 274 49

So Precious 51
Ragged Ear, the Rabbit 52
Deer At Home 54
Animal Behavior 58
Monday 59
The Silent Desert 60
Cold Fish 62
Evolution at the Bay 64

Preface

From furry tumbling kittens to steely eyed mountain lions, animals have an amazing effect on human beings. We love our pets and are in awe of wild animals. Every living thing from insects, to birds, to elk inspires us all in nature. But with developments encroaching in the desert, swamps, and mountains and stress on our climate from mining, fossil fuels, and pesticides, humans are not only endangering animals, but also ourselves.

Animals are part of nature—urban, rural, and wilderness. The relationship between animals and humans is uncanny. We have emotional ties with these creatures and animals have emotional ties and needs of us. We have found ways to make animals work for us in so many ways. As animals become endangered and extinct, what does that say about our chances for survival?

Culturally, animals have entered into our folklore, history, and fables. Their use in stories has helped primitive cultures to explain the events and ways of the world. Besides stories, animals are symbolic and symbols are a strong force in human cultures.

All of these things make up the relationship we have with animals. This is a collection of animal tales that have been part of my life.

—J. R.

THE COMMON MOURNING DOVE

Who coos for you, Mourning Dove?
Who coos for you?

The rabbit watches silent, as you
swoop down to the ground.
The lizard blends into a rock, from him there is no sound.
The desert rat, he does his jig, the snake, he curls a'round.

So, who coos for you, Mourning Dove? Who coos for you?

4/29/12

Falling from a Dark Sky

Dog was sleeping in a drift of sand. It was warm from the afternoon sun. He was sleeping soundly. All around him, the air was a black velvet. There was no moon. The Palo Verde tree wheezed a soft song from time to time.

Then, *splat, splat*…something fell from the sky. Dog stirred his legs. *Splat*. Near his nose. It smelled hot! He woke and jumped up. Nothing. He laid down to snooze. Splat, splat, ping! Something hit the metal awning. His head was alert and he smelled the air. Splat! A hot rock landed on his back—like buckshot on his hide. He scurried up on his feet and looked around in the black night.

He barked a warning. "Hey now, hey now! I've been hit by a rock! Who threw that rock?" No one answered and he settled down to sleep.

His eyes got heavy. *Ping. Ping. Ping.* The rocks hit the awning again and rolled off like marbles. Dog's eyes were wide awake by this time. He looked up in the clear, black sky and could see some blurry stars, but some were bigger and brighter and coming right at him! "Watch Out! Watch Out!" He barked to the night. Dog scurried up the stairs and onto the porch. *Splat, splat…ping, ping, ping. Rattle, rattle, rattle.* He woofed under his breath at the noise. One more outburst of rocks and he was going to bark into a frenzy and wake up his human! Suddenly, there was silence. He circled around the welcome mat, stretched, and went back to sleep.

In the morning, Dog's human, Bill, came out of the mobile home and watched the sun rise with a cup of coffee in his hand. He stepped over Dog. He sat down on the steps and Dog came over to him. Bill gave him a pat and a scratch. His eyes looked down on the steps and he saw a lot of burnt black and brown gravel. He picked up one of the rocks and examined it. A rooster crowed to welcome the sun.

Bill whistled, then said, "Wow, Dog, I think we had a meteor shower last night." He held out the rock and Dog sniffed it. It smelled a bit like burnt metal.

"Good thing you slept on the porch. You could'a gotten pelted by one of these things."

Dog barked. "I did! I did!"

CHOCOLATE BROWN RABBITS

I crunched down the desert trail, excited to breathe in the fresh warm air and hear the musical birds all around me. I told Carl that I had to go out and he said to go as he pulled the twisted aluminum away from our wind-blown porch. I rushed to the desert near the school and then, as I came around the corner of the trail, I stopped.

Twenty eyes were watching me: all standing straight and tall on their haunches with their ears in the air. At least ten rabbits! Now, these were not gray cottontails that nibbled in our yard in the morning or early evening. They were not jackrabbits, with their tan and gray coats with black tinge. They were brown. Chocolate brown. Shorthaired, velvet, chocolate brown. Almost that burnt umber brown in the large Crayola set. They matched the clay-colored soil and the rocks on the top of Golden Gate Mountain, which loomed in back of them. They all had Little Orphan Annie Eyes. They were oval in shape and the eyes looked like they were all going to cry in a blank sort of way. My brain said "They are not real," but I was watching them breathe; their little chests were heaving ever so slightly. I could see a whisker tremble here and there as they breathed. Each rabbit was just a bit bigger than a jackrabbit, but they were very different. They reminded me of some old souls of some ancient time, only here for a brief rest.

Naturally in my haste to get out to the desert, I did not bring my camera. I just stood there frozen, not daring to move. Two of the big ones became hesitant—like they sensed they should move on and then: "Weeeeeeee! Yayyyyy!"

Kids started pouring out into the nearby schoolyard with their high-pitched screams and yells. The large rabbits let out a cross between a chirp and a squeak and they were off like a shot with the younger ones behind them in a whirl of red dust. They were swift and they bounded over large-branching Cholla cactuses in a single hop. I was hoping they would circle around like the jackrabbits do or that I could keep up with them with my eyes. They were heading diagonally towards the end of the Tucson Mountain Range to the west where the ancient native trail would take them across the Arva Valley to the center of the universe at the peak of Baboquivari and down to the Mexican border.

Now, some people thought I saw a migration of rabbits from one seasonal spot to another. Other people wondered if I was seeing things. Perhaps these were jackrabbits with winter coats? Who knows? But I did see something, and they were chocolate brown rabbits.

LITTLE BROWN FOX KNOWS

Little Brown Fox knows that when he comes up from the creek and the deep, dark woods, that there is a gravel road. It is so bright there in the blazing sun that he has to blink his eyes—one, two, three,—to be able to see. His orange and brown fur bristles into a ruff, like flames from a fire. He sees a car just up the road rolling slowly towards him. He stares at the car and the car stares at him. Little Brown Fox hears high sounds, like a young pup. Little Brown is skinny as a rail, he stretches his neck out, flaps his ears, and shakes his skinny legs. Then he turns and trots down the Parrett Mountain gravel road, followed by the slow car. After bit of trotting, Little Brown knows there is a corner with oak trees growing in it. He darts off the road there at Bob's Corner and cuts across the stubble field.

JUNE REYNOLDS

Shadow and Shade

September 4, 2016

I live in a house that was built for a Korean War veteran. The family lived there for decades and before they left the house, they had some big dogs. They even had a hand-built kennel. I think the dogs might have been poodles.

One evening as the sun was setting, out of the corner of my eyes something was moving in the living room. I looked down the long hall, and at the end of the hall framed in the doorway, some dark matter flashed before my eyes. There was a shadow of prancing paws. There was a flappy ear!

The next night, I saw a shadow of something in the living room, prancing like a hobby horse with paws clacking on the hardwood floors. There was a scurrying of a second shape of a shadow, then nothing more.

Days went by and out on the front porch, I saw a shadow in the shade. I blinked my eyes, thinking I was seeing things. There it was again. That did it! I went out and chased it all around. The screen door opened in the wind and soon there was another dark dog-like shadow prancing about.

I see them once and a while. Silhouettes of the past. They are nice dogs, happy dogs, but dark. I gave them names; they are Shadow and Shade.

They are ghost dogs.

Sentinel Cow

A dusky peach light slowly envelops the night sky and the orange spotlight sun hikes its way over the twin peaks. Sentinel Cow climbs the ridge on this morning from her warm, soft bed in the sand from the wash. She looks back on her growing twins, still snoozing on the ground. She is the lead cow on the range in these parts, but she is not the only one in the sixty-square-mile land.

Slowly, she picks her way up the slope, around the cactus and yuccas. Finally she reaches the top and smells the breeze. She stands one way and looks down. She stands the other way and looks up. She quickly gazes at the water about twenty miles below. It was a nice summer down there. Now it is turning to fall. The breeze is not warm, it is cold.

She sees a handful of her kind on one side of the hill so she follows the ridge to be in line with them. There, in a fold of the land, she finds a tender Palo Verde with branches that the deer have missed. She hungrily bites them off with a mighty snap. The next branch is higher and she cranes her neck up to the sky. She wraps her tongue around the branch and…snap. It is off, and she is munching the sweet juicy leaves. Then she nibbles daintily on the other side.

Crunch, crunch, crunch. Suddenly, out of the corner of her eye she sees movement. She turns both eyes at the movement and sound and stares head-on. She sees two hikers. They are coming over the opposite ridge. She normally sees hikers on the hiking trails or roads. They are never this high on the hill by the water truck. Only one has a stick, but she is not holding it like a gun. They are not hunters—they are hikers The two are walking on the ridge and one is wearing a flappy hat that is blowing in the cool breeze.

"Mooooooo!" She sounds the alarm. She moves away from her succulent tree and plows down the ridge. The young calves and their mothers scatter. They know something is happening. Some see the hikers and stare. The young ones dance around this way and that, flinging their heads around and kicking their hind legs like bucking broncos.

Sentinel Cow watches. She now sees there is no danger. The hikers keep hiking through on their ridge, glancing over and taking a few pictures. The little calves are racing down the hill and into the wash. She feels that they are such foolish creatures. She does her duty as she marches between the calves and the hikers, trying to marshal some order.

Owls

People think that I collect owls. I do not collect owls. They collect me.

I think this all started when I was ten years old and my Grandmother, Olive Weisenback, gave me a rhinestone owl pin. I wore it so much, the pin broke free from the owl. The glittering bird rattled around in a jewelry box until I got a music box from my Great Aunt Bonnie (Weisenback) Hagg. It was an old-fashioned dusting powder box with a music box that played "The Yellow Rose of Texas." I took my owl and glued it on the lid of the box with a big glop of old liquid cement. That owl has been on the top of that box for decades.

So my Grandmother spread the rumor that I collected owls. She found or made many of them for me. There was no criteria for good or bad owls. Foam owls, pine cone owls, glass owls, owl curtains. My Great Aunt gave me a used old owl purse which may or may not have made it home or maybe it just rattled around in the car for many months, I don't know. It is not that I am ungrateful for owls. They are thought of as wise and all-knowing. They are thought of as protectors of people. They are magical.

The owl may be my spirit animal. For a few months when I was in high school, I went down into the woods at least once a week, to do a biology ecology study. In the fall, each time I hiked down, I would hear sounds. Something big was flying and making creepy, strange noises up in the looming tree branches. The sounds became more and more intense and were very spooky. They would echo from one side of the narrow creek canyon to the other. I was pretty frightened. I scanned the high canopy of the trees looking for the echoing sound. It seemed to get closer. Then, there is was! A gigantic bird with a ghostly face looking down and chatting at me! It was a barn owl. I saw him a few more times and he never made any more sounds. He would just sit silently on his limb and stare at me. Sometimes he would get bored and fly off to the barn in the next hayfield.

Many decades later, my son and I found spotted owls peeking out at us from the centers of overgrown Christmas trees. They were tiny and looked like feathered, almost rodent-like critters with bulging eyes. Their feathers were covered with spots, but everyone told me that spotted owls did not live in Christmas trees.

Years later, we were hiking on the Mackenzie River and had the pleasure of an owl meeting us at a trail/canyon crossing and he followed along with us for a couple of miles before we lost him. Now it is common to have all types of birds follow us on trails as we hike.

So as you see, owls have crossed my life many times. I never have shared this entire owl thing in public. I never complained about this owl confusion, but I may have made the wrong face one day. It was the day when my Grandmother Olive came into our house with a roll of something. "June, June," she called. "Guess what I found?"

I looked carefully. "A map!" I guessed.

"No it's owl wrapping paper!"

My owl collection 55 years later...

COYOTE

Coyote was making his way across the desert. Zigging one way around a stand of cactus, zagging another way around the rocks. He found Prospector Trail and followed his nose to the Whiskey Wash Bar. He decided to go in. It was as dark as a cave. His eyes got used to the dim light and he hopped up to the bar and put his paws on the flat wood.

"What can I do fur ya, stranger?" said the barkeep.

"I'll have a drink" said Coyote.

Well, this was Whiskey Wash Bar, so when a customer says they will have a drink that means they want whiskey. So the barkeep gave Coyote a shot of whiskey. Coyote lapped it down then said, "That little bitty glass was not enough! I want a saucer!"

So the barkeep gives the Coyote a saucer of whiskey.

Coyote laps it up. The water was burning like fire on the coyote's tongue.

He is now so thirsty that he falls off the barstool and crawls out the door.

"Hey, wait a minute, pard'ner," yelled the barkeep. "In this saloon, you gotta pay!"

"Ah, did YOU pay the clouds for the water?" asked Coyote.

"No," said the barkeep, without thinking. Everyone else laughed.

Coyote walked outside on that note. That was the worst-tasting water he had ever drank. *What is wrong with this place*, he thought. *It really was not like the desert.* He wished that he could go back to the desert. He almost ran into a saguaro because he was blinded by the sun. He forgot he had been in a cave it was so bright! He wandered around up and down many paths with tin tipis on either side. "Look at that scroungey dog!" said a little girl. *I am NOT a dog*, he thought as he trotted along.

The sun sunk low into the mountains and soon the sky was purple and dark blue.

Coyote came to a fence and on the other side there was grass, sand, and a pool of blue water. He climbed through the fence. Coyote rolled in the grass, did his business in the sand, and then jumped in the pool of blue water. A man yelled, "Watch out Walter! There's a Coyote in the water hazard! Get the groundskeeper, Bill!" The men jumped up and down and waved sticks with funny round mallets on the end. Coyote ignored them and drank the water. He stood in the water and let his fur get all wet. It was cool, and when he got out, he took half of the water with him. Soon there were all the yelling men and a groundskeeper in little carts that puttered around as they chased Coyote all over the grass and sand, until he found a hole in the fence that went out into the desert.

I am not thirsty any more, but I sure am hungry, he thought. Then he saw a fat rabbit. "Rabbit," he said, "how did you get so fat?"

The rabbit did not trust the Coyote, but he told him her secret anyway. "I sneak up to the man's porch each night and eat the dog food put out for the dog."

Coyote nodded. "Oh," he said, "that sounds like a very good idea." He only said that to put the rabbit at ease. He had no intention of going back to eat at the man's porch. He knew that rabbit, by habit, would not go on her way but circle 'round to see if Coyote took her up on such an idea. So Coyote turned back just a bit to see if rabbit would also circle 'round. And when she did, Coyote leaped in the air and came down on the rabbit and ate her.

After all was digested, Coyote took a bit of a nap. That water at the bar not only made him thirsty, it also made him sleepy. The whole night he slept under a mighty saguaro with many arms.

The next morning he woke up to the doves cooing. The sun was rising through a prism of puffy clouds. He looked up to see a blazing white church. The lighter it got, the brighter the church became until it looked like it was on fire! He was so weak and dizzy he could hardly walk. He knew if he could get past the church there was a café where he could order menudo to calm his stomach and head, so he dashed over the rocks and past the flaming church, to a wide, hard road where cars were whizzing by, and then…

Proud Bird

March 26, 2016

Cardinals are such proud birds. Today, the male sat atop the highest mesquite in the neighborhood and started singing as he tottered on a swinging branch from on high:

Doreen doreen doreen doreen!

His wife sat down below in an impenetrable bush and chirped:

Eep eep eep eep.

This exchange went on for ten minutes, then there was a huge fluttering in the bush. Then silence.

The male Cardinal looked down, then swaying on the uppermost limb started singing:

Rio rio rio! Rio rio rio! This went on for 15 minutes.

The eggs were laid and he was now a proud Father!

Up the North Umpqua

*C*rack, crash, crack! The silence of the forest was shattered high up in the crown of an old, craggy-limbed Douglas Fir Tree. My eyes shot up to the top which was moving wildly despite the stillness of the air.

Then there was a drifting of daffy down baby bird quill feathers, like flakes of snow, wafting and floating, end over end to the trail below. I could see a large mother bird looming over the cracked limb plucking feathers from the messy nest. More white feathers swirling down to the ground. More rustling. A baby bird appeared over the broken limb. His eyes grew wide as he tried a gargled caw. He looked down, then ducked to the womb of the nest.

Woosh, woosh woosh.... The regal father arrived. He looked as fearsome as any United States Eagle on any logo. He perched precariously on the broken limb and demanded to know why his egg-let is not up on the edge of the nest. The baby popped up again and gazed over the ground forty feet below. He peeped like a chick and ducked down to his Mama. There is some Motherly cooing.

By this time I am sitting down right in the middle of the trail to watch the show.

Father does some wild flapping and fills the forest with a very loud caw. The baby popped up, then another and another. Fuzzy feathers are flying everywhere. Father gives each chicklet a love peck. There is some giddy hopping high on the rim of the nest. Father looks, then swoops, and dives ten feet from the trail. Then he loops back up to the cracked limb. The eaglets are teetering on the edge as Mama climbs up to the nest-edge. She unfurls her wings and flaps them. The chicks do the same. Dad springs from the limb and soars around. The limb finally cracks and falls. It gets caught on a smaller tree below. Mama flies down to a flat limb ten feet away. Father comes in for a landing on another limb, which bounces up and down. The first eaglet flaps both wings, dives, and flutters to the Mother's limb. The other babies flutter their wings and flap like miniature ducks to the landing limb. Father caws. Mother caws. The babies peep. They all fly up to the nest in an awkward flutter and Father flies away. The flying lesson is over for today.

SURPRISE IN THE MEADOW

Swirling ground fog boiled up out of the Alsea River that Saturday morning as my Dad and I crossed it. We were glad that the rest of the runners we going to meet wanted to start early. Dad was going to take the truck after the run and go to Philomath to get lumber. That meant that we would go to the Mexican cafe and have big, juicy burritos and tacos.

We went up the Alsea Highway and swooping around all the curves. Missouri Bend, Blackberry Campground, and up to Alsea. There we turned off and crossed the river at the town of Alsea, Oregon and went up to the falls. The rest of the guys came from Highway 20 and somewhere up there we all met. There was an eight mile trail that we could train on up there. A good, rough, cross-country trail.

Stretching and warming up, we joked around about the run. All the runners were pretty tall and some were practicing for college meets or marathons. When we took off, we looked like a bunch of galloping horses. It was not a completion but I wanted to jump out ahead of everyone for the practice and the joy of being alone. After the first half-mile, I cruised along. Then, out ahead I saw that the trail forked. We had been reading poetry in high school and that Robert Frost poem about the two roads in the woods came to mind. As I got closer, I saw that the road not taken had been taken by something big early this morning. There was a muddy track of prints and fresh brush and ferns smashed down, so instead of taking the main trail, I took the other.

It was interesting and pleasant with the morning sunrays cutting through the leafy trees. The flashes of light through the flailing alders reminded me of a disco ball, you felt like you were moving more than you really were. I was dizzy by the light and movement. I just kept on going until…*thud!* I ran right into a body. Standing upright. It was the hind end of a young elk. He hopped a bit to one side and looked at me. He was huffing at me and his eyes were wide open, like he was going to take me in. He was young but twice as big as me. I was a bit freaked out by the sight. Out there, the whole meadow was a sea of elk. They were steaming in the sun and it smelled like a barnyard. It was a bit frightening being among these animals. I stood frozen as the elk closed in around me, milling silently this way and that.

Then I heard an elk moo sound followed by the snort and saw two really big boys with horns coming at each other. This must be the rutting season and these two bucks must have been the kingpins. Sure enough, they charged at each other with a crack of horns. They tangled together for a few seconds, then they untangled and came apart. They backed up for the next round. The other elk were agitated and milling around, so I took advantage of their movement and skirted through the meadow weaving my way through the herd. I saw an opening on the other side which was sort of a drain for the lower end of the grassland. I crashed through the ferns and hoped I would find the other trail. (That was about the time I wished I had not taken the road less traveled.)

Pretty soon, I heard some talking and saw the runners. Flecks of their bright running gear splashed through the trees. I got back on the trail and caught up with them. I was very relieved and grateful to be back.

At the trailhead, one of the guys came up to me with a question: "Hey Rhy, I thought you were ahead of us."

"Aw, I was, but then I started thinking about poetry and took the road less traveled. I ran into an elk herd." I looked down. My legs were splattered with mud and elk dung.

My friend laughed. "That's what you get for thinking about poetry, man."

My Dad was amazed. "You saw an elk?"

"No, I actually ran right into the back end of an elk and a whole herd of elk in the meadow. They were so big and powerful, that they scared me." I explained.

My Dad the tree planter, was familiar with these woodland adventures. "Hmmm. Must be rutting season. Did you see any horn clashing?"

THE CHICKEN FEEDING SONG

Oh, come a' runnen'
come a' runnen'
come a' runnen'
Oh, come a' runnen' to me.

Oh, come a' runnen'
come a' runnen'
come a' runnen'
Oh, come a' runnen' to me.

I've got gold in my pocket, in my pocket
Oh, come a' runnen' to me.

I've got silver in my saddle, in my saddle.
Oh, come a' runnen' to me.

I've got lead in my shot gun, yes my shot gun.
Oh, come a' runnen' to me.

I've got turkey in my oven, in my oven
Oh, come a' runnen' to me.

BIG CREEK PIGEONS

There are many Big Creeks, Lost Creeks, and Beaver Creeks in Oregon and I think that I have been to them all. Every creek has a story that may, or may not, be told. I was camped above Big Creek in an unidentified location where these birds, like pigeons, were causing quite a stir. They reminded me of the birds who used to live in and flew out of barns, swooping the sky. Farmers called them "roller pigeons." But this flock was wild and out of control, fluttering wildly in the tree branches. On closer inspection, I saw that they were feasting on the berries of the Cascara Buckthorn or *Rhamnus purshiana*. In the Native American Chinook language, it was called "chittem," which was the first word I learned for that tree. People would harvest chittem bark for a laxative.

I asked Cal, the owner of this woodland property about these pigeons: "What are these birds?"

He looked at the tree fluttering with a huge flock, bending over some of the willowy limbs. "Uh, bird, birds…"

I could tell by those shifting eyes and his twitching mustache that he was holding back information.

I placed my hands on my hips. "Well, they look like someone's barn pigeons that have gone wild."

He just followed the birds with his eyes, as they left the tree. "May-be."

The birds fluttered in groups of twenty up the hill and dive bombed-the tops of their favored trees. Soon the ground, bushes, rocks and, Lord forbid, our white camper was speckled with purple bird poop. Indigo bird poop—very deep and ink-like.

"So Cal," I begin again with our woodland steward, "Where did these birds come from?" There could only be a handful of people over the last thirty years who could be responsible for these birds gone wild.

He shook his head and said, "Dun-know."

So the mystery remains. I did some research and one of the interesting scientific things I learned is that the gorging of these ripe berries by the birds has no ill health effect on them at all, except for the birds being a bit overexcited and deranged.

Two years later on my quest to solve this mystery, Cal's wife who is a native of the South Oregon Coast says that she has always known these birds as "Band Tail Pigeons" and they are wild and a not a domestic bird. Case Closed.

Oregon Bear

By Lyle Kent

Bear floated down Dairy Creek from the Coast Range Mountains. He found an old drift log and rolled it down the bank of the Tualatin River. Well, as you know, the Tualatin River means "slow moving," so it took two months for him to get down through the valley. Finally, he got tired and jumped off the log and onto a trail. The trail got bigger and bigger and there was four lanes this way and four lanes that way with hard, shiny horses zooming this way and that. *Well this is a strange place!* He thought. *Where are all the other animals, and especially bears?* There were hard ribbon trails criss-crossing over and under each other. He got so dizzy looking at it that he fell off the track and ended up in a black field which was filling up with the hard horses. The rain was turning to snow and he thought he would seek cover. He saw a huge square cave and decided to duck in. It looked like the general store that he sometimes used to see at Rose Lodge, only lots bigger! Soon he saw a big picture of green and blue mountains and letters on wood like at the General Store. The letters were R-E-I. He didn't know what they mean. He couldn't read. He waddled into a cave within a cave and saw all kinds of things from the woods; trees, bushes, grass, and hiking boots. There were also tents and fake fires. There were people all around, but not many animals. A little boy and little girl ran up to him to pet his fur. That felt nice. So he licked the little girl. She tasted like honey! The girl and boy screamed and ran away.

In the middle of the store was a huge Doug Fir tree that towered overhead to a cliff. *Why lookie at all the pretty little stars shining through the limbs,* marveled Bear. The tree was full of strange balls, and funny stuffed men in red suits, blue suits, and striped suits, and dollies, and bears, and red and white swirley canes and hiking sticks. He climbed about halfway up the tree. He bit into some of the canes but they didn't taste good so he threw them on the ground. That is when some men started yelling: "Hey, YOU, get down from there!" Women started screaming. Boys and girls were crying. *Why are they so sad? Why are they so scared? This is such a nice tree. I can be the shining-bear star swinging up here in this tree!*

He smiled down of the crowd of people bearing his pretty, white teeth. Everyone screamed again. *They really like me.* He thought.

He climbed up level with the cliff that had people on it and they were yelling too. Then he saw a cliff on the other side with a big cougar standing there staring at him. He roared a greeting at him, but the cat just stared. Everyone else heard him because they roared back, screaming in their people voices. He jumped off the tree and on to the cat's cliff. The cat seemed friendly, so he took a nap right next to the cat. As he drifted off to sleep, Bear thought he could hear the cat purr.

Purrr Purrr Purr Purrrrrrrrrrrrr. What a nice cat, thought Bear.

But then Lyle woke up!

Striker, the house mouser was snuggled next to me. He was purring loudly. I thought, *Man, I need to quit having these folktale dreams.* I think I'm going crazy.

Message

Jettisoned dart that streaks the yard.
High-pitched urging by messenger bard.
He calls to his mate with a whistling word:
"There's food on that limb." Says the hummingbird.
Urgently whisking from tree to tree
Zipping, safe passage for all to see.
He has a secret for you and me.
Secrets of life in the air so free.

DEVIL DOG OF REX HILL

Let me tell you about the Devil Dog of Rex Hill. You know, that steep hill on 99W between Newberg and Sherwood, Oregon? Many people have stories about that dog, going back to the days of the Model T. He would even stare down the engineers on the trains at the Rex Hill railroad tracks. Some say he was a "left- out-in-the-rain" dumped dog." He is still seen after all these years, so of course, he is a ghost. A special kind of ghost that people call a Devil Dog.

In the 1990s—I can't remember which year it was, but it was between one year and another because it was New Year's Eve, I was coming home from a family party in Newberg. I had borrowed my Grandma's 1976 Grand Torino and I was bombing that boat of a car up the hill by myself. It was raining furiously. At the top of the hill, I could see that it was socked in with fog. There is a bit of a bend in the road as I burst into the fog bank, and there, right in the center of the highway in front of me, was a big, black dog! He pranced into my lane like a hobby horse, his ears flapping.

The outline in my headlights made him look like he might be some sort of Doberman. The ears, head, and body were black, but there were golden tan highlights. His eyes were yellow and glowing and he barred his pure white teeth at the car's lights.

Braking the car, I could not stop. I slammed on the brakes and they sunk clear to the floorboards. I was afraid I was going to hydroplane on the road, so I carefully braced myself with the steering wheel. I did not slide or turn—I just kept going straight. There was no giant bump of dog that I expected to run over. I did not hit anything. It was if I just ran right through him.

I looked into the rear-view mirror to see the dog standing in back of me. He was standing in the exact space, in the same lane, that I had just come from! He had turned around and was facing me. That gave me chills down my spine. I was now stopped in the middle of the highway and his eyes were glowing red in my brake lights. The motor of the Grand Torino was still humming as if nothing happened. The dog came running at the car and I lifted my foot off the brake and accelerated. The dog kept running in back of me. I sped up, and he kept up with me. I slowed down and he stayed right in back on me, galloping along. Then finally, a car came the other way and the spell was broken, or at least I thought it was.

But that Devil Dog spirit followed me home. As soon as I walked into my house, a table near the door fell over, as if an animal brushed by, knocking all the books and papers onto the floor. Later, I found the hall rug all crumpled up on the floor. My cat's water dish was dumped over almost every day for a month. I emptied several cat food bags and wondered why my cat seemed to be eating for two. All of the pictures that I took in the house came back with some sort of orb flashing in it.

Of course, my Grandmother who lives with me found out about the dog right away. She said she saw it. "Get that pesky dog out of here right away," she ordered.

I sighed. "There really is NO DOG."

"Don't lie to me boy!" she spat.

I got caught up in one of our crazy arguments. "You can hardly see the TV how can you see an imaginary dog? Huh, Filbert? Huh?" I called her Filbert when I was mad.

"I see that dog with my nose. I can smell that dog with my own eyes a mile away!" she declared.

"Okay, Filbert." I wanted this argument to end. I told her the whole story and she was not surprised. Still, she wanted the dog out of the house.

We brought in a psychic from out of town to access the situation.

"You DO NOT get rid of a Devil Dog," she declared. "No, never. You ran over him, you get to keep him. It's your responsibility."

I was in denial. I shook my head. I could not believe that adult people were so crazy. "No, no. Since when has a ghost been anyone's responsibility? This is a figment of our imagination…how can we have any responsibility over that?"

"I got it!" cried the psychic. "You can name the dog Rex! Get it? The king?

For Rex Hill? Maybe he won't like the name and leave."

So I paid the psychic for a name for a dog that doesn't exist and for her to leave.

"Waste of money!" shouted Filbert as the Psychic left.

At that time I lived a pretty boring life and I think that the Devil Dog, Rex, got tired of my routine life and returned to Rex Hill. Finally, I didn't have to mop the floor around my cat's dish, she went on a diet, and things were not scattered around the house. The Devil Dog was very spooky, but I always felt sorry for him in a strange way.

(This story is dedicated to the storyteller, my friend, Brady Gage who passed away on March 31, 2018 at the age of 43. We worked together for ten years at Sherwood High School and he was a loyal worker and creative partner. He befriended many teachers and students and was working with others to make a superhero coalition to help children suffering from deadly diseases. He will be missed by so many people in two communities who took joy in life and those who were in much need of joy and happiness.)

Dark Raven and the New Ocean

By Lyle Kent

I am Dark Raven. I was once a child who lived on the Big River. But one day, I fell in the Big River and would have gone to live with the Salmon People if it wasn't for another raven who swooped me out of the river and changed me into a raven too.

I learned to fly long distances and see the world way past Big River to the Rock Mountains and all the way west to the ocean. The ocean was bigger than the river or any of the Klamath Lakes and it always roared. I could fly over all the mountains or land in the lowest river marsh. I would bring the news of the land to all the animals and people.

One day, I was sitting on that Mountain right over there. They now call it Wild Horse Mountain, but long ago it had no name and was not as tall.

I was sunning my dark green, iridescent wings in the morning sun, looking to the east, perched on the tallest Doug Fir around. Then, I heard a rumbling. I looked to see if the mountain I was on was moving, but the sound came from the east. It sounded like the ocean roaring. I flew toward the sound and got to the place where Big River and Long South River came together. The water was swelling, then churning, then rumbling with large rolling boulders.

There were floating chunks of ice, looking like ferry boats, carrying pink and gray chunks of granite on them. This scene was most curious. There had been no big rains in months. Where was all this water coming from?

I saw a human running from the water and I swooped down and carried him to the top of a steep ridge. He was yelling thanks, but my attention turned. I could see that there were many people and animals being swept by the water. Some were washed right up to the ridge and they clambered onto the rocks and trees as fast as they could go to get higher on the mountain. I looked for humans in trees, bears on rocks, and deer on hillocks and tried to fly them to safety. Finally I was back to the mountain I had come from and tried to warn the animals there. Some ran up the mountains where the natives lived in the summer. I swooped up as many humans and animals as I could. Soon, the water filled the deep creek beds and then swoosh! A tide of water, rocks, and ice chunks with boulders, all flooded the ground. Just as I thought the water would go over the lip-ridge of the mountain and over into the deep valley, there was a slop. My big mountain grew up and a big hand rose up from the mountain to stop the water. Large waves of water roared and the earth shook. The water bounced back away from the mountain and streamed back the way it came.

I was so tired, I flew up to my big Doug Fir to watch the most amazing thing. To the north and east, I could see all that water swirling, in five or six whirl-pools going around and around. Some of the animals shouted "It is over! It is over!"

I crowed "No! No! Do not go down! Stay up here! Stay up here!" Most of the animals did stay, but some were foolhardy and curious and raced down to the muddy, rocky land below. They were caught in the mighty whirlpools with huge trees that were stirring the mud into a chocolate pudding. The valley to the east was a sea of water. Only the great white headed mountains who were lovers of long ago held their heads above the flood.

The next morning, there was another swoop of water barreling towards the mountain ridge. It was not as deep as the first, but the land was changed in one day from deep valleys cut by babbling creeks to wide-open, muddy plains filled with deep layers of rocks and mud. Over on the other side of the mountain there was not as much water; but the Long South River that swung around the mountain was flooded for a very long time.

The humans on the south side of the mountain were saved from the flood. I guided the humans that survived to the other side of the mountain. The humans had to be helped because they are not as sturdy as the animals, but at the same time, they make songs and dances that no animal can do. None of us will never know why the ocean of water came from the east and we hope the ocean of the west will stay its banks. It was a curious event.

The Peccary Parade

Ajo, Arizona has a new civic pride and mission in their dusty old town that mining forgot: It's the Peccary Parade! Every evening before sundown when the horizon is blue on top and pink on the bottom, in that drowsy light, a line of javelinas—a furry dog-like pig—of its own species comes a'walk'en, single file, sideways across the mountain. They magically squeeze through any number and types of fences. They trudge along like they've been out on a long day's job—no doubt in some javelina mine.

Finally they make their way to a dry wash located in a burro corral. The Burros watch in stunned relief, counting the marchers in a line, as the sun goes down to the west for the night.

Morning is announced by the bray of the lead burro. An asthmatic sputtering: *Auuuuuu heee-haaaaw, augggg hee-haw! The* sun pops up from behind a peaked mountain and then, deep in the shadows, a line of javelinas march down the steep rocky wash, through the corral, and through the fence. They follow the early morning shadows across the RV Park. Their line swerves through camps with water bowls and dog food. Each bowl is upended with a loud clatter. The elder of the line chastises the clumsy teenager. The line is broken up by the disturbance.

The clatter and snarling alerts the humans who come out to photograph the parade. This time, the javelina are very peppy, marching their hooves on the cement with a uniform tap. There are twice as many animals today, since it is a weekend and a javelina holiday.

Each peccary looks curried and combed for the event. They are the healthiest javelinas that I have ever seen. The baby is licked by his mommy because his hair bristles will not lie down. Oh, of course when he gets to the iron gate, he goes through and the hairs get all messed up again.

Later and a mile down, at Millie's Roadrunner Donut Shop, people are crowding by the windows to witness the parade.

"WHEN are they going to come?" Asks one of the ladies.

A man sighs. "They'll be here soon Madge."

And sure enough, on the other side of the highway, one block away, we see the parade of peccaries march through the avenue. We see each one as they go by and we count them. There are twelve all together, including the baby.

"What a herd!" another man exclaims.

Millie laughs. "They will be back by nightfall."

The Black Lizard

Who should I meet, after bake-oven heat?
The Lizard is out with the spiny tail
His skin is rumpled, his tail is crumpled.
He needs bugs to eat. His tongue is so neat.
He scurries around with a scratchy sound.
'Till he crawls to the edge of the shade and sun.
He gobbles two flies and his meal's begun.
Later I stand and I catch his eye.
He scrabbles away—there is no goodbye.

June Reynolds

Sheep 274

"And this news just breaking...Sheep 274 was terminated today in the Catalina Mountains."

Yes, I was on that rocky crag last night. I was right up on top of the saddle of Tucson Canyon. I perpetuated the murder of said sheep—mountain goat to be exact. I had not eaten in three days and I was weak. It was twenty-six degrees or so that night. I was hunkered down below a very cold cliff, shivering.

Suddenly, just above me, I heard a crashing of brush and rocks rolling down the hill. I heard a grunt and a maaaa. She slid off the cliff on her hind and plunged down the hill to my side. She did not scramble up. She laid there in a heap. Easy prey. I jumped up and lunged at her throat. Her eyes were so big I thought they would explode. She held up a broken leg, snapped in two.

I drug her about twenty feet down the hill to another rock outcrop and had my warm dinner. One by one, two by two, lights sparked the valley below. It was mesmerizing. The night was cold and clear, but I was full and warm.

Sliding sideways, the morning sun beamed and warmed up my nest. My big wet tongue cleaned my face and paws. The sheep laid in a hump to one side. I took a bite and my tooth hit a hard black thing. The thing cheeped like a bird. I tore that thing from the sheep and it rolled down the hill. After breakfast, I roamed down the canyon to some pools of water. The water was snowmelt and was crisp and cold. I looked up and there was two little sheep looking at me from the ridge above. They were stock-still, but I could see that they were trembling in fear. No need, I thought. No need.

After lunch, I felt energetic and ready to move on. I thought I would move west to the next rise of mountains. The sun sunk to the west and the moon glowed to the east. A pack of coyotes were hovering over on the next ridge smelling my kill. I had a last bite, cleaned up, and moved up to the saddle of the canyon again. I would follow the trail down by the light of the moon. As I topped the final ridge, the coyote pack howled a happy dance before advancing to the sheep.

I am the Puma, the Mountain Lion, or you can call me a Cougar. I am in the mountains and on your doorstep.

So Precious

Unfolding her wings in a patch of morning sun.
She flattens them softly to dry.
Wild thunder and drowning rain have not destroyed
The beauty of her fragile life.

Ragged Ear, the Rabbit

Ed Dart and I were standing by the fence, jaw-jacking about our Gold Flower Road neighborhood. Above, in the clear-blue sky, we saw two large hawks circling overhead.

Ed gave a whistle. "This is quite a year for hawks. I've seen more than I've ever seen."

"And rabbits." I added.

Ed chuckled. "A year or two ago, one of the baby bunnies just dropped from the air in my driveway. It was an early mornin' and there was a whole litter of babies all over the place. One of those hawks dive-bombed a poor little creature, caught it up in his talons, and flew just over that mesquite tree over there. That bunny was a-dangling there and kicking his legs up at the bird. He was flailing his whole body around and then, plop, he just fell out of the sky. His ears and head were pretty bloody and I went out to check him out, but when he saw me, up he jumped and ran away."

I nodded my head. "I've seen that rabbit. We call him Ragged Ears and I wondered what happened to him."

"You think he is still around?" said Ed.

"Yep, I saw him this morning. He is a bit skittery but he has come back three days for some rabbit pellets. He always hangs out in the shade and looks nervous.

Ed smiled. "Well, I'll have to look for him now and see what he looks like. You say his ears are all chewed up?"

"They look like velvet rags," I said.

DEER AT HOME

Here I am in the acorn trees.
The desert oak, among the bees.
This is my home, it's where I've been…
Please be sharing and keep it clean.

JUNE REYNOLDS

This is my young'un, pride and joy.
He's my little, springing boy.
We nibble here, we nibble there.
We roam the canyons with never a care.

But watch out! Warning!
There roars a car.
That is where the dangers are!

JUNE REYNOLDS

My eyes are brown and my light coat dark.
Thank you folks for staying in our park.

Animal Behavior

Hare–Erect
Rabbit–Alert
Coyote–Wander
Cougar–Steel-eyed gaze
Cow–Stomp of disapproval
Hummingbird–Aerial Stunts at warp speed.

Monday

Monday is bird bath day.
Such drinking. Such splashing. Such showing of wing!
As they flutter out,
They dry high in the branch of the willow.
In puffy pecking order.

THE SILENT DESERT

Silently… even the air is quiet. Black velvet night warps around the air. It is so quiet, you can hear it breathing. It is not noise you hear. It is nothing. Soothingly, nothing.

Long after midnight the moon rises through a crack in the mountain range. This light alerts the coyote pack to howl in their various locations and group together on their hunt.

Silence

Asthmatically, there is a far-off *crrrhooca hoo* (wheeze) ahhhg hoo ca hoo.

A chipper, short report: *hoot hoot hoot*. There is a flapping and then: *Cooohooo coo ahh hoo cooo hooo coo ahh hoo.* More flapping.

Silence

Moaaa-ca, moaa-ca. Two legs scurry on the wash. The moaning sounds like a small dog, ending with the sound of a choked-off bird. *Moaaa-ca, moaaa-ca.* Then a wild dash of feet in the gravel.

Silence

Moon has moved overhead, spilling out its silver light onto the desert. Suddenly, out in the wash, there is a marching sound and an occasional clip-clop of little hooves over the bedrock. *Crunch, crunch, crunch, crunch (never ending), crunch, crunch, crunch, crunch*. Military drill style, coming from the canyon of the wash. *Grunt, grunt!* (March out of step…) *Crunch, crack, snap, crunch, crunch.*

The crunching meets something big, loud, and kind of crazy: *Heee haw hee haw ahhh (wheeze) heeeee haw!* Galloping of many hoofs. Trotting of one lonely great grandson of a Wild Mule left out in the desert by the miners years ago.

Silence

The sickening baby scream of a dying rabbit in the maw of a Coyote. He drops his dead prey. *Ow ow owwwww! Ow ow owwwww!* Coyote back-up of the solo: *Yip yip yip yip ow ow owwww!*

Silence

Moon sets into another mountain range. *Cooo coo coooo coo softly crows* the sleepy Cactus Wren, before she realizes this orb is sinking, not rising.

Silence

Cool air from the mountain canyons, streams down to the desert floor and sometimes makes a whispering *woosh* through the Palo Verde trees. Slowly it becomes lighter as the sun climbs the mountain range. The velvet night unwraps to the west and takes the last of the silence with it to new lands far away.

Cold Fish

(This is a futuristic, cautionary tale of animals gone a-wry. Oh woe the new-found animal. We should have been more careful with our environment…)

I found myself at the Oregon Coast on the beach of my childhood, possibly near Rockaway Beach. In those days, the beach houses looked more like whitewashed shacks, all tilted at angles in the drifted sand. The sky was a very blue backdrop to the creamy white hillocks and the peeling white buildings. The windows were curtained by faded multicolored beach towels.

Suddenly I heard a squeaking of moving metal and a screech of metal on metal in measured rhythms. It was sounding from the side of the tilted shack. I looked around to the building to see some ungodly thing moving up and down, up and down, up and down, bearing towards me.

"What the heck is that?" I exclaimed.

"A cold fish." A deadpan reply. I jumped. My son was beside me. I did not realize anyone was near me.

The old thing gleamed in the sun. It was an old walker, long ago abandoned by an immobile elder, which was now humping its way up a sandy ridge. When it got to the top of the ridge, it looked to one side in profile and I realized the unreal creature had a yellow plastic bowl attached on a stick for a "head" and a pair of barbeque tongs for a "beak." They would snap from time to time. There was some sort of bicycle handles for arms.

My son, who is an addict for science and nature programs on TV, continued his commentary. "This is called a cold fish. He's like a hermit crab who gets in a shell or whatever in which to live."

"The dead fish gets into the walker?" I asked.

My son laughed. "Yep. But the fish is not dead. He is alive. He fills all voids in the seat the bowl, and the tubing. Sometimes the animal is a collective life form, but we refer to it as a single one. He is a viable new life form. He is a modern adaptation of nature."

My mouth flew open as I gasped. "That is just too creepy."

He sighed. "It's the way of our world now, it's not too bad yet. But when these garbage islands move in off the ocean and onto our beaches, we may be in for a big surprise."

Suddenly something came crashing over a dune on the other side of the shack. It looked like he was following the first cold fish who just kept on moving out to the ocean. This new, crashing cold fish looked more like a rust bucket, revolving on three legs, flapping a grill off the side. It was faded red and I realized it was an entire barbeque. The lid was ajar and several skewers were sticking out of what could be imagined as a mouth.

This piece of junk somehow knew we were there because he revolved very close to us, scraped up a spatula of sand, reached out, and offered it to us.

My son pushed the spatula away and said, "No thank you." The rust bucket turned to me and offered me the spatula of sand. My son stifled a laugh as I nodded and said, "Thank you, sir."

EVOLUTION AT THE BAY

But the story did not stop, for the next day, I was down at the Alsea Bay. It is a small bay which snakes around and has a strong bar as the river water pushes out into the ocean. There are plenty of deep pools and sandy bar for the seals at low tide.

I went up to the docks, not far upriver from the bay. At the end of the street there you could park and rent some crab pots and get crabs right off the dock during the right season. I rented a couple of crab pots and some bait and the guy at the dock sort of looked at me funny. He shook his head and took my money.

I was pretty excited as I flung my first crab pot into the bay. It plunged right down then drifted a bit under the dock. I managed to get the second crab trap farther out and it swung out to the ocean. Off in the distance, I could see a white object. It started sailing right at me from the center of the current. That seemed a little strange. In no time at all, the white thing was bobbing right in front of me. It zipped right up to the dock and submerged.

The day was three shades of blue and was dazzled by twinkling water sparkles. A faint breeze made the water choppy and the American flag waved a limp flap.

Kersploosh! A slap of water washed onto the dock and the white lumpy thing exploded up out of the water with my crab pot! It was empty.

Now I could see this white lumpy thing clearly. It was a mass of gallon milk jugs somehow lashed together with wire, rubber bands string, barbed wire, long grass and yarn. There were masses of pink guts in those jugs. It was a colony of cold fish. I cringed at the sight of the pink squirming guts and realized that this mass of protoplasm with a mild jug shell had just sucked the bait out of my crab pot. No wonder the dock guy looked at me funny when I said I was going to get crabs for dinner!

"Pretty pathetic crabbing, right?" said someone behind me. I jumped, but it was only my son, the nature lover, again. I looked at the milk jug mass bobbing right off the dock.

My stomach turned as I took a stick and pushed it back away from the dock.

"The ocean is so full of garbage that it is choking the natural flow of life. Now life is in garbage and soon it will overtake humans." He said grimly. "There will be no life on the water, except for cold fish and, as you have seen on the beach, the cold fish are evolving onto land like the first animals long ago."

"People do not believe that there is climate change or that the oceans are engulfed with garbage," I said

My son coughed. Little pink protoplasm balls fell out of his mouth. "We have missed the boat…miss the boat…. miss the boat."

"Wake up Grandma! We are going to miss the boat!" The voice was my grandson, by the bedside. We were going out on a fishing boat. The whole sickening story was really a dream, but could it really happen?

www.ingramcontent.com/pod-product-compliance
Lightning Source LLC
LaVergne TN
LVHW020436080526
838202LV00055B/5223